By Apple Jordan
Illustrated by Robbin Cuddy

First published by Parragon in 2012
Parragon
Queen Street House
4 Queen Street
Bath BA1 1HE, UK
www.parragon.com

ISBN 978-1-4454-4751-3

Printed in China

Bug Stew

A little story for little learners

Bath · New York · Singapore · Hong Kong · Cologne · Delhi
Melbourne · Amsterdam · Johannesburg · Auckland · Shenzhen

Timon and Pumbaa
love bugs.
Yum!

Simba learns to
like them, too.

Time to hunt
for more bugs!

The friends go
and find a few.

They look under rocks.
They look up in trees.

They find fat flies.

They find bumblebees.

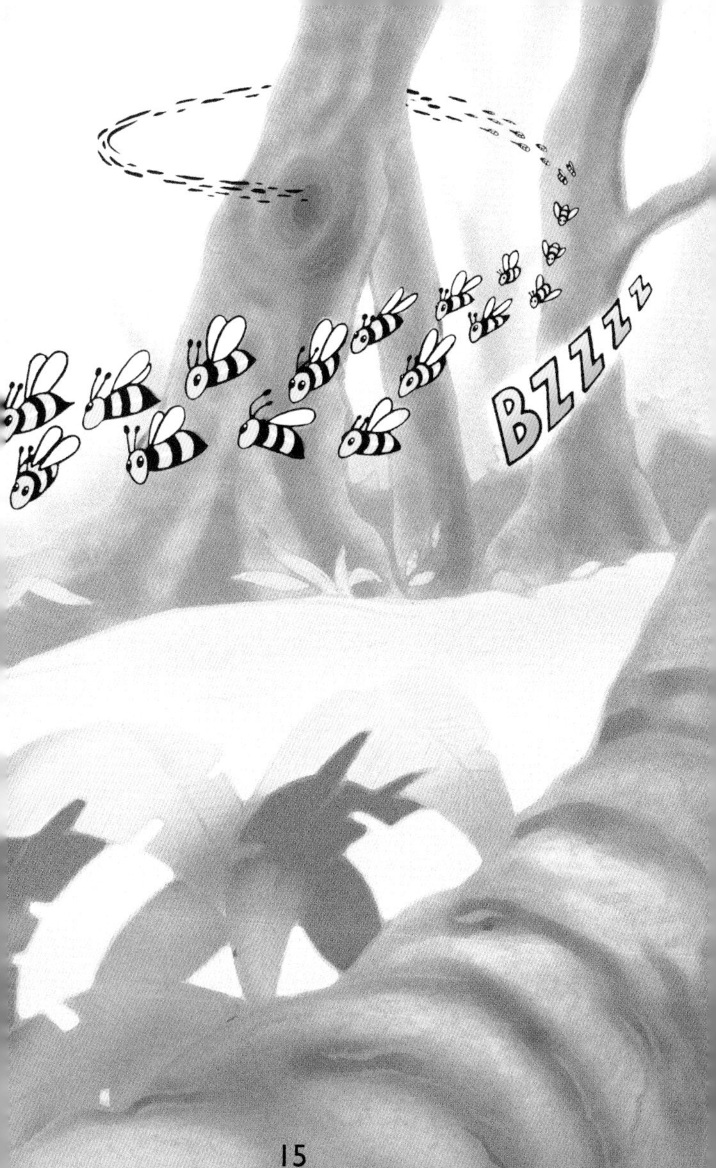
BZZZZ

They look inside logs
for slimy slugs.

They look and they look
for all types of bugs.

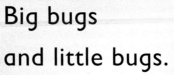

Big bugs
and little bugs.

Crunchy bugs,
sticky bugs.
Chewy, gooey,
icky bugs.

Bugs that can sting.

Bugs that can fly.

Bugs that run fast.

Bugs that crawl slow.

Bugs that can swim.

Bugs that can glow.

They have
buckets of bugs.
Now what will they do?

Mix them all up
and make a bug stew!